FISHING
FOR PETS

AND OTHER STORIES

STARSCAPE BOOKS BY DAVID LUBAR

Novels

Emperor of the Universe
Flip
Hidden Talents
True Talents

Monsterrific Tales

Hyde and Shriek
The Vanishing Vampire
The Unwilling Witch
The Wavering Werewolf
The Gloomy Ghost
The Bully Bug

Nathan Abercrombie, Accidental Zombie series

My Rotten Life
Dead Guy Spy
Goop Soup
The Big Stink
Enter the Zombie

Story Collections

Attack of the Vampire Weenies and Other Warped and Creepy Tales

The Battle of the Red Hot Pepper Weenies and Other Warped and Creepy Tales

Beware the Ninja Weenies and Other Warped and Creepy Tales

Check Out the Library Weenies and Other Warped and Creepy Tales

The Curse of the Campfire Weenies and Other Warped and Creepy Tales

In the Land of the Lawn Weenies and Other Warped and Creepy Tales

Invasion of the Road Weenies and Other Warped and Creepy Tales

Strikeout of the Bleacher Weenies and Other Warped and Creepy Tales

Wipeout of the Wireless Weenies and Other Warped and Creepy Tales

Teeny Weenies: The Boy Who Cried Wool and Other Stories

Teeny Weenies: The Eighth Octopus and Other Stories

Teeny Weenies: Freestyle Frenzy and Other Stories

Teeny Weenies: The Intergalactic Petting Zoo and Other Stories

Teeny Weenies: My Favorite President and Other Stories

TEENY WEENIES

FISHING
FOR PETS
AND OTHER STORIES

DAVID LUBAR

ILLUSTRATED BY BILL MAYER

A TOM DOHERTY ASSOCIATES BOOK
NEW YORK

This is a work of fiction. All of the characters, organizations, and
events portrayed in this novel are either products of the
author's imagination or are used fictitiously.

FISHING FOR PETS AND OTHER STORIES

A Starscape Book
Published by Tom Doherty Associates
120 Broadway
New York, NY 10271

www.tor-forge.com

The Library of Congress Cataloging-in-Publication Data
is available upon request.

ISBN 978-1-250-18783-3 (hardcover)
ISBN 978-1-250-18784-0 (ebook)

Our books may be purchased in bulk for promotional, educational,
or business use. Please contact your local bookseller or the
Macmillan Corporate and Premium Sales Department
at 1-800-221-7945, extension 5442, or by email at
MacmillanSpecialMarkets@macmillan.com.

First Edition: May 2020

Printed in the United States of America

0 9 8 7 6 5 4 3 2 1

For Brian Selander,
who never ceases to amaze me as he finds
new ways to make the world a better place.

CONTENTS

FISHING
FOR PETS
AND OTHER STORIES

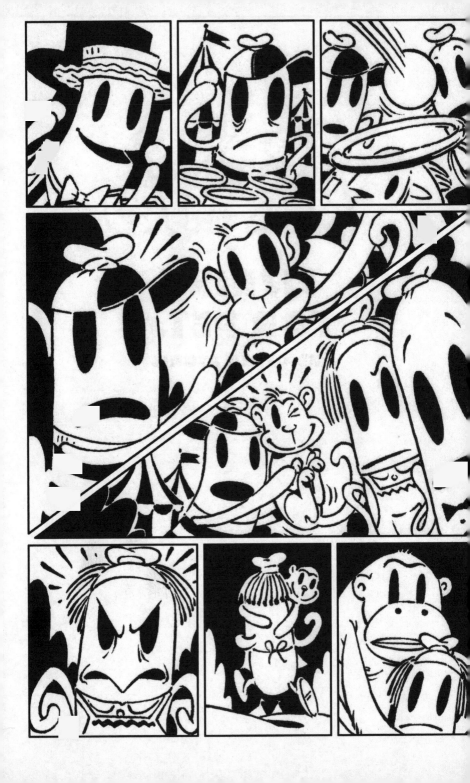

FISHING FOR PETS

I never win anything. I don't know why I even try. But I really wanted a goldfish. And you could win one at the carnival just by getting a Ping-Pong ball into one of the small bowls stacked up on a table. I tried and I tried, but they kept bouncing off the edges.

"I give up!" I shouted. I hurled my last ball at the bowls as hard as I could. It smacked one on the rim, shot straight up, smacked the top of the booth, shot back down, bounced up again, then fell into a tiny golden bowl all the way in the back.

"Winner!" the guy in the booth shouted. "You win the grand prize! Nobody has done that in ages." He bent over and reached under the counter.

"I just want a goldfish," I said.

Before I could explain anything more, he straightened up and plunked something warm and furry into my arms.

I stared at it. It stared back.

"That's a monkey," I said.

"Yes, indeed," the man said. "And you are one lucky kid."

"But . . ."

I tried to think up the best way to explain that my parents would never let me bring home a monkey.

"Tell them you won it," the man said. "We're closing up in an hour. We'll be gone by the time they come back. They'll have to let you keep it."

I wasn't sure I wanted to trick my parents. But how could I say *no* to my very own monkey? I really couldn't.

On the way home, I decided to name him Snickers, because that was my favorite candy bar. He seemed to like that.

"Look what I won!" I said as I walked into my house.

Dad stared. Mom stared.

"That's a monkey," Mom finally said.

"I think you're right," Dad said.

"Take it back," Mom said.

"I can't." I looked at the clock on the wall. "The carnival is closing soon."

"We'll see about that," Dad said. He grabbed my hand and headed out the door.

I clutched Snickers and raced along next to Dad. The carnival was still open when we got there.

"We want to return this monkey," Dad said.

"Sorry, all prizes are final." The man pointed to a sign that pretty much contained those same words.

"I don't care what the rules are," Dad said. "Take back this monkey."

The man leaned forward. "I'll tell you what. I really can't do that. But here's what I'll do." He held up a Ping-Pong ball. "I'll give you a free play."

Dad snatched the ball out of the man's hand and flung it past him as hard as he could. "I don't want a free play!"

The ball smacked into the rim of one of the bowls, shot in the air, bounced off the ceiling of the booth, smacked another bowl, and another, and then rolled around the rim of a final bowl three times before falling into the water.

The bowl was golden. So was the water.

"Winner!" the man shouted. "Wait right here." He dashed behind the booth.

"Run," I told Dad.

But before we could skitter away, the man came back holding hands with a small gorilla. And a small gorilla is a very big animal.

"I don't—"

Whatever else Dad was going to say got cut off as the gorilla leaped into his arms and gave him a kiss on the cheek.

We staggered home.

Mom was not pleased.

"We'll see about this," she said as she stormed off toward the carnival.

"I hope it's an orangutan," I said as I watched her leave.

"A gibbon would be nice," Dad said.

She came back with a goat.

PACK RATS

The Wykowski triplets, Edith, Mercy, and Rhea, were struggling up Bard Street. Three things added to their struggle. They were the smallest kids at Chester Burnett Elementary School. Bard Street was the steepest street in town. And Bard Street was the only way to get home from school. They'd received new textbooks for all of their subjects, and had to take them home to get covered. Bent under the weight of their backpacks, they fought for every small step.

Brawler Einhorn had no trouble walking up the hill. He was the fifth-strongest kid at

Chester Burnett Elementary School, and could have almost carried all three Wykowski backpacks, along with all three Wykowski kids. But Brawler wasn't the helpful sort. Quite the opposite, he was a bit mean. (Some of his classmates felt this was caused by his failure to even make the top three when it came to strength.) He was also in a bad mood because he'd had to stay after class to get a lecture about paying more attention.

So he started out way behind the triplets. But he caught up quickly enough as he plowed his way toward the top of the hill. He could have passed them and kept going. But their struggle caught his attention.

He walked past them, then turned around.

"What's the matter?" he asked, using the sort of voice one would use with a baby. "Too heavy?"

The triplets nodded, all at once, in a slow and creepy way. They stared at him, unblinking, with identical grim expressions that would have given a bit of a chill to anyone who actually paid attention to other people.

Brawler laughed. "Weakling," he said, poking Edith in the shoulder.

It wasn't a hard poke, but Edith was already off balance. She let out a gasp as she toppled backward.

Brawler let out a laugh. He hadn't expected such a rewarding and amusing sight. "Next?" he asked, holding up the same finger he'd used to topple Edith.

Mercy shook her head and took a step backward.

That was a mistake. The weight of her pack pulled her back. She staggered for three more steps, then fell, just like her sister.

Brawler leaned forward, putting his face so close to Rhea's, their noses almost touched.

"Boo!" he shouted.

Rhea jumped in the only available direction.

That, too, was a mistake. She followed

pretty much the same path as Mercy, also ending up on her back.

"Hah!" Brawler cried. "That was awesome."

He expected them to quiver in fear, or start bawling. As spooky as they looked, he didn't expect them to point at him and chant.

"Round and round. What goes around comes around. Down and down!"

Brawler frowned as an unfamiliar sensation spread through his stomach. He'd rarely felt fear. Shuddering, he turned away from the triplets and headed for the top of the hill.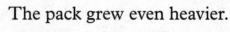

He didn't notice anything at first. Then, another unfamiliar sensation tugged at him. His backpack felt heavy. "It's just my imagination," he said out loud. He hunched his shoulders and continued walking.

The pack grew even heavier.

He looked ahead. The top of the hill was still about fifty yards away.

Each step was harder than the last.

Finally, with the top of the hill just a few feet away, he realized he didn't have the strength for another step.

He tried to take off the backpack. But the straps were digging so deep into his shoulders, he couldn't slip free.

Someone walked past him.

It was the triplets.

"Help!" Brawler cried.

They turned to face him, but didn't say a word. The hill was so steep near the top that the triplets' eyes were level with Brawler's trembling chin.

"Please . . ." Brawler said. "I've learned my lesson."

Edith shook her head. "No, you haven't."

"Not quite yet," Mercy said.

"But soon," Rhea said.

All three reached out toward Brawler's nose with a forefinger and tapped him ever so lightly.

"Yargggg!" Brawler howled as he toppled backward. He hit the sidewalk, and then slid, throwing sparks from the zipper on his backpack as he shot down the pavement toward the bottom of the hill. Halfway down, the backpack burst open. Books and papers spilled out. By the time Brawler reached the bottom of the hill, his backpack was empty, and he was able to get back up on his feet.

Three sets of eyes watched from the top of the hill as Brawler started to make his way back up. On the way, he gathered up his spilled possessions and crammed them into the backpack.

"That was fun," Rhea said.

"I hope he learned his lesson," Edith said.

"If not, we can try again next time," Mercy said.

"In that case, I hope he *didn't* learn his lesson," Edith said.

They all laughed. Then they turned away from Brawler and headed home.

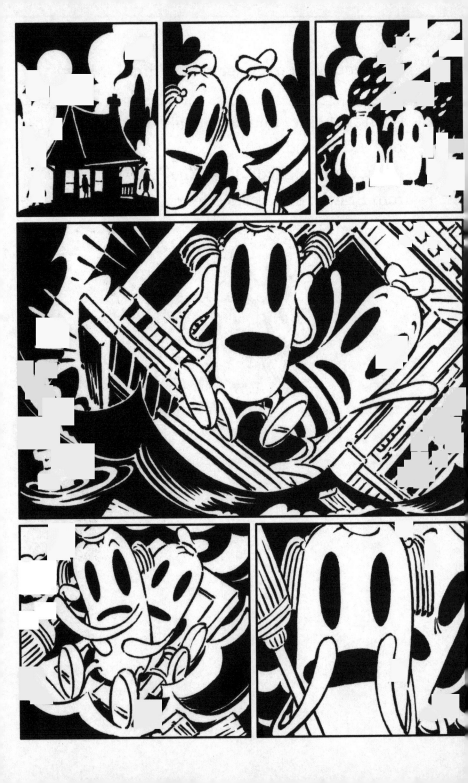

RISING WATERS

Lisa's father paused at the door and turned back one more time. "Are you sure you're okay with this?" he asked.

Lisa nodded. "We're fine. Go ahead. It's not like we're little kids." She wished he'd stop worrying. That just made her nervous.

"We'll be right back," her mom said. "We want to get some groceries before the storm hits."

"Who's in charge?" Lisa's twin brother, Dennis, asked, looking up from the fishing reel he was cleaning.

"Both of you," Lisa's mom said. She glanced

toward the sky, then said, "We'd better hurry."

Lisa watched her parents drive down the dirt road to the bridge. The car crossed the river, then climbed the hill toward the highway that led to the grocery store. It was noon, but heavy clouds had turned the world dark as an unlit basement. "Nobody needs to be in charge," Lisa said to Dennis. This was the first time they'd been left alone at the cabin. At home, with neighbors all around, it was not a big deal if her folks had to run an errand. But here, in the woods by the river, they were alone.

"Something could happen," Dennis said. "Then I'd have to be in charge, because I know all about the woods. I was a Scout, and you never were."

"Okay," Lisa said. "If we have an emergency and we need a fish caught, the job is yours."

Dennis started to say something, but his words were blasted away by a flash and a boom. Before the echo of the thunder had died in Lisa's ears, another harsh sound filled the air. Heavy rain was falling, smashing the ground as if an ocean had been overturned and dropped from the sky.

Lisa shuddered and stepped back, closing the door. *I hope they're safe,* she thought, wondering if her parents had reached the store yet.

"Big storm," Dennis said.

"Big storm," Lisa agreed, "but it can't last long." She looked out the window. Some- thing was so wrong that, at first, she didn't even see it. When she realized what had happened, she gasped. The bridge was gone from sight, covered by the river. An angry, churning rush of water was spilling over the banks, rising to the dirt road, racing toward the cabin.

"We have to get out," she told Dennis. *But where?* Her parents were across the river. The bridge was underwater. There was nothing behind them but flat woodland. It would all be flooded if the river continued to rise. "Maybe the roof," she said, thinking out loud. Lisa looked out again. The water was higher, lapping at the ground just a few feet from the cabin.

"Don't be silly," Dennis told her. "We'll be safe here. The river can't rise that high. It's never really flooded the cabin."

"Never?" Lisa asked.

"Nope." Dennis pointed to the wall near the floor. "See where the color of the wood is different? That's as high as it ever went. And that only happened once. Dad told me it was back when he was a kid. So relax."

"Okay." For a moment, Lisa felt better. But she couldn't help looking out the window. The river didn't seem to know it wasn't supposed to go much higher. It was moving toward the cabin at a steady rate. The rain fell harder.

"Dennis," Lisa said, walking to the couch, "take a look. The water is almost here."

"Don't worry about it." He didn't even look up.

Lisa returned to the window. As she looked out, she gasped. Everything was happening too quickly. The water was already over the three steps that led down from the front porch. She opened the door to look out.

"Keep that shut," Dennis said.

Lisa closed the door, hoping the solid piece of oak could hold back the water. Outside, the river lapped against the base of the door. A small trickle leaked inside, but the seal was fairly tight, so not too much got in.

The thunder had moved past them and was now rumbling in the distance, but the rain continued. Lisa knew the river was not going to stop rising. She had to make a decision. "Dennis, we need to do something, and we need to do it now. Take a look at this."

Dennis gave her an annoyed stare and walked to the window. He looked out, and then he looked down toward where the rising water beat against the cabin. For a moment, he said nothing.

Lisa waited, then she asked, "What should we do?"

"I don't know."

"We have to make a decision," she told him.

He shook his head. "We'll just stay here. Everything will be fine."

"No." She scanned around the small cabin, searching for anything that could help them. There was a couch, a couple of beds, and a small table. She looked at the door again. The river slapped against it, an unwelcome stranger demanding to get in. She realized the river was about to get its wish.

"Help me," she said, running for the toolbox her parents kept in the hall closet. She came back with a hammer and screwdriver. She used the tools to knock out the hinge pins from the door.

"What are you doing? You'll let the water in," Dennis shouted.

"It's our only chance." She pulled at the door. "Help me," she said again.

"But we can't—"

"Help me!"

Dennis pulled with her. The old oak door finally came free with a shriek and a groan. Water burst through the opening, quickly claiming the cabin floor. The door twisted in their hands. "Let's get it outside," Lisa said.

They wrestled the door to the porch. Lisa reached back and grabbed the broom. "Drop the door and get on top of it," she said.

Dennis followed her orders. They leaned the door over, then let go. It hit the water, sank for an instant under the force of its fall, then bobbed on the surface of the water. Lisa and Dennis climbed onto the rocking platform. The water was still rising. Looking back, Lisa saw it was already a foot deep inside the cabin. She could actually see it climbing the walls.

Lisa used the broom to push away from the

cabin. In an instant, they were moving with the current and there was no chance to change her mind. "I hope I made the right decision," she said, wondering whether panic had driven her to make a serious mistake.

Dennis got a strange look on his face. "You were right," he said, pointing behind them. Lisa looked back. Again, what she saw was so wrong that, at first, she didn't really see it. The cabin was leaning. It was giving in to the force of the water. In another instant, with a cry of ripping wood, it was torn from the ground and swept away.

A moment later, a light sliced through the dark, catching the two of them as they clung to the door on the river. "Lisa?" a voice called. "Dennis?"

"Here!" she shouted. There was the sound of an outboard motor. She saw her parents, along with the man who owned the store. In another moment, Lisa and Dennis were climbing into the safety of the boat. She watched as the door was carried away by the water.

"We were so worried," her mother said. "But I knew I could count on you kids. You did the right thing."

Dennis shook his head. "Lisa did the right thing," he said.

"Thanks," Lisa said. She huddled against her parents as the boat took them across the rising waters to safety.

THE WISH LIST

"Class, let me be the first to wish all of you a wonderful summer," Ms. Barjani said. "I hope you have all made lots of wonderful plans."

I had. I planned to play baseball, go swimming, and just hang out with my friends. I looked at the clock for the five hundredth time that day. Ten minutes. And then, summer vacation would start. I turned my attention back to cleaning out my desk. After I got the last pencil stub and permission slip out of there, I felt around to make sure I hadn't missed anything.

"What's that?" I said as I felt something small and cold. I pulled it out.

"Yeah, what is that?" my friend Franz asked, looking over my shoulder from his seat behind me.

"Stupid magic wishing mirror," I said.

"Why's it stupid?" Franz asked.

"It doesn't work," I said. I remembered when I'd opened the package. My great-grandmother in Slovenia had sent it to me. There was a note saying it was a magic mirror that would grant any three wishes I asked for. It was a Christmas present, but it arrived two weeks late. I had a big test the next day, and I hadn't studied, so I held up the mirror, stared into it, and said, "I wish it would snow so much that school is closed for a whole week."

It didn't snow.

I failed the test.

I was going to toss the mirror away, but then I thought maybe if I wanted to close the

school, I had to make the wish at
school.

So I brought the mirror
with me and waited until a
good time to try it out. When
I heard that picture day was
coming, I pulled the mirror from my desk and
said, "I hope it snows so much that school is
closed for a month." I hated the way Mom
stuffed me into a suit and nearly strangled me
with a necktie for a stupid photo.

Naturally, I didn't get my wish.

"You sure it doesn't work?" Franz asked.

"Yeah. Watch." I held up the mirror, and
after glancing at the clock, where I saw we
still had five minutes to go, I said, "I wish we
were outside right now."

"Thanks for including me," Franz said.

I didn't answer him. I was too busy wondering why my hand felt so warm. The mirror was
heating up. It started to vibrate.

"Whoa!" I said as I dropped it on my desk.

Words appeared on the surface of the
mirror:

Wish queue filled to capacity. Wish fulfillment activated. Processing the first of three.

"Huh?" I was slow to catch on.

"What's a queue?" Franz asked.

"It's stuff in a line, like in a Pez dispenser, or a pack of Life Savers," I said. "Or us, waiting at the cafeteria."

"It's snowing!" someone shouted.

Everyone looked out the window. Snow was falling hard and fast. I glanced down. The roads were already coated. In minutes, it looked like more than an inch had fallen.

I remembered my first wish. I'd asked for so much snow that school would be closed for a week. It looked like I was getting my wish. But we were getting closed in, not closed out.

I guess about three feet of snow fell.

A new message appeared on the mirror.

First wish set in motion. Processing the second of three wishes in the queue.

The snow got heavier. I realized we'd be getting a month's worth. Or a week and a month, depending on how the two wishes were combined. I couldn't even guess how high the snow was. I thought about being trapped in the building for a month. Or a month and a week, if the wishes didn't overlap. That's when I realized all I had to do was wish away the snow.

I reached for the mirror, just as the words changed.

Second wish set in motion. Processing the third of three wishes.

And, like that, I was outside of the school, standing on top of a ton of snow, wearing shorts and a T-shirt. Franz, who was next to me, let out a yelp. So did I.

Somehow, we got back into the building.

It was not a good summer.

THE
HAUNTED CAMP

It was quite a bargain. Colton's mother couldn't resist. The ad in the newspaper caught her attention early in the spring of that year; at the top, the words GRAND REOPENING! were spread across the page. Beneath that, a subhead that was only slightly smaller read *Give your child the gift of Camp Spruce Glen!*

There was more, in a smaller font, proclaiming the reopening of this abandoned summer camp that had been closed for so long that Colton's mother had never heard of it. The description sounded great, and the price was amazingly low.

When Colton heard the news, he couldn't help shouting, "Yes!" He'd been begging to go to summer camp ever since last year when most of the kids he knew had gone. But those camps had been wildly expensive. So he'd had to settle for hanging out at the playground that summer, and at  the town pool with the other kids who hadn't gone to camp.

"This is great," he said.

"It will be a wonderful experience for you," his mother said.

Had they known the rumors about Camp Spruce Glen, they might have been a bit less enthusiastic. But Colton didn't learn anything about the rumors until the day he got there, and his mother never heard the rumors at all.

"Looks like it could use a bit of sprucing up," Colton's father said as the family drove along the entrance road for the camp.

Colton didn't get the joke. He was too busy

looking around at the cabins, the lake, and the fishing pier to make the connection between *Camp Spruce* and *sprucing up*. And even if he'd paid attention, he was not a big fan of his father's jokes.

His parents dropped him off with a hug and a kiss on the cheek, and Colton went to meet his fellow campers.

The very first kid he approached greeted him with, "This place is haunted."

"What?" Colton asked.

The boy, who was tall and thin, with thick glasses, a collection of freckles worthy of playing connect-the-dots, and a name tag with *Darryl* scrawled on it in dark blue marker said, "There's a ghost. People think it was an old trapper who broke his leg in the woods and died when he was trying to crawl into town for help."

"Oh," Colton said. "Okay . . ." He didn't believe in ghosts. Not a whole lot, at least.

"I read all about it," Darryl said. "That's

why the place closed. Campers kept disappearing. One of us is going to die. I'm pretty sure of that. It won't be me."

Colton looked around for someone else to talk to. As he walked toward a small cluster of campers, Darryl followed him. "Stick with me, you'll be safe. I know all about paranormal manifestations."

Colton had no plans to stick with Darryl, or anyone else who tossed around words like *paranormal* and *manifestations*. But it turned out they were in the same cabin, along with Marshall, who was good at sports, and Norman, who cried the entire first day and well into the night.

The crying wasn't enough to keep Colton awake that night, but the sudden slam that shook the cabin was more than enough to wake him.

"Depart!" a voice cried.

Two other sleepers awoke, disoriented and startled, joining Norman, who was already awake, and Colton. They leaped from their bunks and switched on the lights.

Colton walked over to the wall where the noise had come from. He looked out the window. There was nothing to see. All lights were off, and the clouds filtered out the light of the half moon.

"Someone's playing a joke," Colton said. "That's all it is."

"Yeah," Norman said, nodding.

The boys went back to their bunks. There wasn't another thump that night, but other strange and disturbing things continued for the rest of the week. Objects disappeared from the cabin. Twice, dead animals were awaiting them in the cabin when they returned from evening campfires. Cold night air would flood the cabin as the door swung open.

Colton didn't believe in ghosts, but he also didn't believe in spending all night feeling scared. He called his parents and told them he wanted to come home. They told him they were at the beach and he'd just have to make the best of things.

The thumps came back. So did cries of agony that made Colton's skin crawl. Finally, toward the end of the second week, he decided he was going to catch whoever it was that was trying to scare the campers. As soon as they turned out the lights, he sneaked out of the cabin and hid behind a tree on the side of the wall that had been the target of most of the thumps. The moon wasn't up yet, but the stars were bright, and he was pretty sure he'd see anyone, or anything, that approached the cabin.

Sure enough, less than an hour later, a dark figure slipped out of the woods and glided toward the cabin. He moved so smoothly that, for an instant, Colton feared he really was watching a ghost. But as the figure moved closer, Colton saw it was just a slim man strolling along the path with the grace of a dancer.

"Got you," Colton whispered.

He thought about jumping out, but decided it was better to follow the man to see where he went.

The man banged on the cabin. He raced from there to the other cabins, giving the wall of each one a hard thump. Then he turned and fled back into the woods. The slightest sound of feet on the path, along with the thumps his fist had made, told Colton the man was truly not a ghost. He followed the sound, hoping he could keep up.

But he didn't have to keep up for long. Five minutes into the chase, he stumbled to a stop. The man was standing right ahead of him on the path.

Colton's gut churned as he realized he was alone with someone who had been terrorizing a whole camp.

"I wish you hadn't done this," the man said. He spoke with a quiet snarl.

"Why are you trying to scare everyone?" Colton asked.

"To protect you," the man said.

That was so unexpected, Colton just stared for a moment before replying. But he also relaxed a bit. If the man wanted to protect them, no matter how strange a method he'd picked, he wasn't dangerous. The moon had finally started to rise, revealing a man who didn't seem to be a threat. He looked like the guy at the corner store back home who worked behind the deli counter.

Colton figured he deserved an explanation. "Protect us?" he said "From what?"

"Me," the man said.

That single word sent a chill through Colton. "You?"

The man pointed toward the rising moon. "I'm bound to these woods, for reasons we don't have time to discuss. And I'm bound to do terrible things when the light of the full moon transforms me. I've always managed to stay away from the cabins. But every two or three years, some foolish camper would wander into the woods at the wrong time. I had to stop them. So I did my best to make the camp seem haunted. I finally managed to get the place closed, ages ago."

"They just opened back up," Colton said.

The man sighed. "I know. But I suspect they'll close it back down, after you disappear."

"Why would I—"

The transformation happened so fast that Colton never finished his sentence. But the man was right. The camp closed up soon after that, right before the next full moon.

MILK-BOTTLE MAGIC

Lorna felt like a fish in a sandbox. She understood that her mom had a wonderful new job, and she understood why the family had to move, but that didn't mean she liked leaving the city.

"Everything's different," she complained to her brother, Donovan. "And I'll bet it will be even worse once school starts."

Donovan looked at her and said, "Glerble." Then he turned back to his blocks. He was a good listener, but at the age of eleven months, he wasn't much of a talker.

"Yup," Lorna said, "I know I'll hate the

school out here." School would be starting in two weeks. Lorna turned toward the door as she heard her mom walk in. "Do you have to go out tonight?" she asked.

Her mother nodded. "I won't be late. And the sitter is supposed to be very nice. I'm sure you'll like her."

"Sure." Lorna doubted it.

The doorbell rang. Even that was different. It wasn't like the buzz in their apartment in the city; it was a big loud *BING BONG* that echoed through the house. She followed her mom to the door.

"Hello, I'm Mrs. Gunderson," a woman said, stepping into the room so briskly she almost leaped. She looked at Lorna. "And you must be Lorna."

"I must be," Lorna said.

The woman just smiled at this.

"Dinner is on the table," her mom said. She looked at her watch and said, "Oh dear, I'm late." Then she hugged her children and scooted out the door.

Lorna watched through the window as the taillights of her mom's car were swallowed by the night. "It's too dark here," she said.

"What's that?" Mrs. Gunderson asked.

Lorna jumped. She hadn't realized that the sitter was right behind her. "It's too dark. There aren't any lights."

Mrs. Gunderson was still smiling. "That just makes it easier to see the stars. Take a look sometime. There isn't a view like that in the city. Now, let's see about this dinner." She left the room and headed for the kitchen.

Lorna trailed after her. Donovan toddled in a moment later. Soon, they were all seated at the table. "You don't seem too happy with Amblington," Mrs. Gunderson said.

"The city is better," Lorna said.

"Things will improve when you start school."

Lorna shook her head. "No, they won't. I'll bet the school here is as bad as everything else. I hate this place. I hate the quiet, I hate the dark." Her gaze fixed on the table. "I even hate these stupid milk bottles. Why can't we get milk in a carton?" She looked at the glass bottle on the table. Her mom had bought the milk from a dairy down the road. The place smelled like cows—like a whole bunch of cows.

"Oh, it's not a stupid bottle," Mrs. Gunderson said. "It's a very smart bottle."

"What?" Lorna had no idea what she was talking about.

"It's very smart," the sitter said again. She poured Lorna a glass of milk, then placed the plastic lid back on top of the bottle. "Watch," she said. Then she put her hands on the bottle and said, "Bottle, will Lorna learn to like it here?"

Lorna just stared, wondering what kind of sitter her parents had gotten. The woman was trying to make a glass milk bottle talk. This was absurd. This was—

BLOOP!

Her thoughts were broken by the noise

from the bottle. The lid rose up a bit, like a trapdoor, then fell back down.

Mrs. Gunderson smiled even wider. "See, the bottle thinks you'll get to like it here. Right, bottle?"

BLOOP, BLOOP!

Lorna didn't believe what she was seeing. The lid popped up and down like a red plastic mouth. "How . . . ?"

"How do you think?" Mrs. Gunderson asked.

"Glerble," Donovan said, giving his universal answer. He pointed at the bottle and laughed.

"Good guess," Mrs. Gunderson said. She looked back at Lorna. "Do you want to take a guess?"

"I have no idea."

"It's very simple," the sitter said. "You just need to remember one fact. First, do you know what *expand* means?"

"Sure, it means to get bigger. Like my stomach expands during Thanksgiving dinner."

"Good. I like your definition. Now, the simple fact is that a gas, any gas, will always try to expand when it gets warmer and contract when it gets cooler. Simple, right?"

Lorna nodded. The sitter continued. "Now, what is in the bottle?"

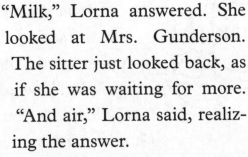

"Milk," Lorna answered. She looked at Mrs. Gunderson. The sitter just looked back, as if she was waiting for more. "And air," Lorna said, realizing the answer.

"Right, again. Now, the milk is cold. And so is the air above it. What happens when I put my hands on the bottle?"

"You warm it!" Suddenly, it all made sense to Lorna. "The air gets warmer, so it expands. It needs more space, so it pushes against the cap. And the cap goes *bloop*."

"I couldn't have said it better myself," Mrs. Gunderson told her.

"That's really neat," Lorna said.

"Glerble," Donovan added.

Lorna felt a bit bad about all her complaining. Even if everything else was no fun in the country, at least she had found a wonderful sitter. "Will you be my sitter again?" she asked.

"Well, I only do this during the summer. I have to go back to work in a couple of weeks."

"Oh." Lorna hated the thought of losing Mrs. Gunderson so soon after finding her. "What kind of work do you do?"

Mrs. Gunderson smiled again. "I'm a teacher. I teach science at the school. It's a good school, and we have a fabulous science program. I have a feeling you'll really like it."

"I have a feeling I will, too," Lorna said.

"Now, if you can get me some baking soda, vinegar, and a balloon, I'll show you something really amazing about gasses."

"Great." Lorna went to get the ingredients. As she moved around the kitchen gathering the items, she glanced out the window at the sky. There were a lot of stars, she realized—stars whose names she didn't know. Not yet.

HAT TRICK

"Come on, Tommy! You're holding us up!" My big brother, Donny, glared at me and shifted the bag of clubs that was slung over his shoulder.

"I'll be right there," I said. I was super excited about getting to play golf on a real pro course. But I was also excited to see they sold Lucky McMurphy golf clothes. He's my favorite golfer. He gets a hole in one almost every time he plays. Nobody is as lucky as he is.

They even had shirts in my size. I looked at the tags and sighed. The price definitely wasn't my size. I'd need a year's allowance to buy one of them. Then I saw the hats.

"Tommy!" Donny's friend Brice yelled as I dawdled by the hats.

"Coming," I said. But I scanned the rack. They had Good Luck hats, Great Luck hats, and just one absolutely awesome Most Excellent Perfectly Lucky hat. I grabbed it and took it to the register.

I didn't see a tag, but how expensive could a hat be?

"Tommy!" Brice's sister, Monica, called. "We can't be late for our tee time."

"Go ahead. I'll catch right up."

The guy at the resister rang it up.

Yikes!

It turned out a hat could be really expensive. It took every penny I had—even the money I planned to use the rest of the month to play at the municipal course.

But I guess it was worth it. Actually, when I put the hat on, I knew it was worth it. I already felt lucky. *Look out world, future pro Tommy Caruthers is about to tee off.*

I hurried to catch up with the others. As I ran to the first tee, the wind picked up. When it was my turn, I took a practice swing, and then got ready to clobber the ball with a perfect drive.

I swung back. The wind gusted, tugging at my hat. I stopped my swing and clamped my hand down on the hat until the gust died.

"Tommy!" three people shouted. "Hurry up."

"You can't rush your swing," I said.

I tried again. And stopped again as another gust tugged at my hat.

On the third try, I managed to complete my swing, even though the wind blew my hat off. But I was so distracted, I hit a hard slice into the woods.

"Bad luck," Donny said.

Brice pointed at the name Lucky Mc-Murphy on my hat. "Maybe you can tell them it doesn't work and get your money back." He let out a laugh like a donkey.

I didn't laugh back. But I smiled when he hit his drive into the sand trap.

I was behind by three strokes on the first hole. I didn't expect to win, but I'd hoped to at least not finish with the worst score.

I did okay on the next three holes, staying even with the others, and moving a point closer to Brice, but the wind picked up again on the fifth hole, and I hit another slice as my hat threatened to fly off. This one went into the lake.

"Refund," Brice said.

As I put down another ball, Donny looked over his shoulder and said, "Hurry up. We're holding up the next group."

"You can't rush golf," I muttered, as I lined up my drive.

By the final hole, I was in last place by three strokes, and behind Donny by five. The only possible hope I had to keep from coming in last was to hit a hole in one. I'd never done that. And this was a par five, which meant there was no way I could drive the ball all the way to the green in one stroke. But the wind picked up hard, pushing at my back.

"Come on, Lucky McMurphy," I whispered, "give me some of your luck."

Even though I knew it was a mistake to try to overpower the ball, I swung as hard as I could. The instant I connected, the wind shifted, and blew my hat right off my head. I heard the ball hit a tree. I heard a cry as the ball bounced back. And I heard the hollow whack as the ball smacked Brice in his empty head. But I wasn't paying attention to any of that. I was watching my hat sail away, back toward the seventeenth hole.

My amazing, expensive, lucky hat was on its way to

the next state. I raced after it. Far off, I heard someone yell, "Fore!" That was followed, two seconds later, by a solid whack as someone hit a drive.

Then I saw the hat jerk in midair, as if it had been shot. My jaw dropped at the sight. The hat plunged toward the ground like a dead bird. As it tumbled, something fell from it.

It was a golf ball.

The ball dropped right into the cup of the seventeenth hole.

The hat fell to the ground next to it.

That had to be the most unfair thing that ever happened to me. When the hat finally lived up to its name and delivered some perfectly excellent luck, it gave it to someone else.

I walked over to the green and stared down at the hat.

A group of golfers approached me from the other side of the green. And I could hear Donny, Brice, and Monica walk up from behind. I glanced back and saw Brice had a big lump on his forehead.

"Nice hat," someone said.

I looked over at the golfer who spoke to me, and my jaw dropped again. I'm surprised it didn't fall all the way to my feet.

"Lucky McMurphy!" I said when I recognized my hero.

"That's me," he said, flashing his famous grin. He knelt and got his ball from the cup. "Thanks for the help. I was afraid I'd go a whole game without a hole in one. No way I'd get one on the eighteenth. That's a par five."

He picked up my hat and plopped it back on my head. "Thanks," I said.

"Listen, kid, I've been watching you," he said. "You've got talent. But you need to work on your concentration. I run a summer program for young players who show promise. You get lessons, and you get to play for free here all summer. Are you interested?"

All I could do was nod.

"Great." He gave me a card with the information. "I'll see you tomorrow."

I went back to the eighteenth green and finished the game. I lost. I came in last. But I was still a winner.

COOKIES
FOR SAM

As the glowing red, white, and blue embers from the last fireworks faded, a great idea hit me. I thought about it all the way home, sitting in the backseat with my younger sister, Trudy. As soon as we got inside, I told her about it.

"I'm putting out cookies tonight," I said.

"What are you talking about, Breen?" she asked.

My name's Breanne, but *Breen* is as close as Trudy's gotten, so far. That's fine with me. There are more important things than names.

"You know how we put out cookies for Santa, right?"

"He loves them. And he brings me presents!" she said.

"So, this is the Fourth of July. It's America's birthday. I'm going to put out cookies for Uncle Sam." I had no idea what he'd give me in return, but I'd bet nobody else ever left him cookies, so he would have to be super grateful.

I hadn't planned ahead, but thanks to Dad's killer sweet tooth, and Mom's love of buying anything she had a coupon for, we had a nice assortment of cookies in the kitchen cabinet. After our parents went to bed, Trudy and I slipped down to the living room and put a plate of Double Stuf Oreos on the table next to the couch. I had a small flag I'd saved from a cupcake last year. I put it next to the cookies so Uncle Sam would know for sure they were for him.

We'd barely made our way back upstairs

when I heard sounds from the living room. We raced back down, and there he was, popping the last cookie in his mouth. He was tall and thin, with a white top hat, beard, and striped pants, just like in the drawings I'd seen.

"Got any milk?" he asked.

"Uh, yeah . . ." I sent Trudy to get a glass of milk.

"Excellent!" He dusted the crumbs from his hands, then plopped down on the couch, picked up the remote control, and turned on the TV.

"What are you doing?" I asked.

"Waiting for my milk," he said. "Oh, soccer! I love watching soccer."

Trudy returned with the milk and handed it to him. "Thanks," he said, not taking his eyes away from the game.

"You didn't bring us anything?" I asked.

"Life, liberty, the pursuit of happiness," he said. "Isn't that enough?"

I wasn't sure what to say. I mean, I was grateful for all of that. But I'd given him cookies. It wasn't too much to expect he'd give me something back in return.

"Hang on," he said. He played with the remote, searched through YouTube, and pulled up an old video. It was a man giving a speech.

"President Kennedy," I said. Our table had place mats with the presidents. I remembered Kennedy from his smile and his hair.

"Ask not what your country can do for you," he said. "Ask what you can do for your country."

I looked at Trudy. She looked at me. We both looked at Uncle Sam. "What can we do for our country?" I asked.

"Just what you've been doing," he said.

"What's that?" I asked.

He pointed at the empty plate. "Acts of kindness. Creative thinking." Then he pointed toward the stairs. "Now, isn't it getting past your bedtime?"

"I guess."

As we headed for the steps, Trudy took my hand and said, "We didn't get a present. He got cookies and milk, but we didn't get anything."

I thought about the gifts he'd mentioned, and I thought about the Christmas presents that were mostly long gone or forgotten. "Actually, we got everything," I said as I tucked Trudy into bed. We had life, liberty, the pursuit of happiness, and, thanks to my parents, lots of cookies. That was a pretty sweet deal.

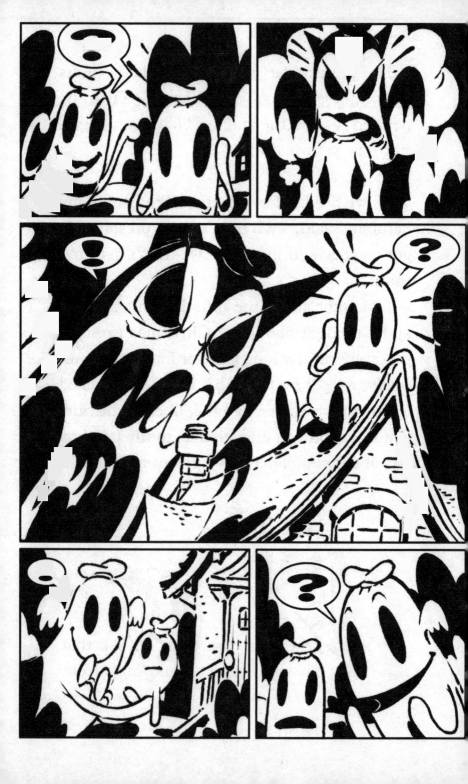

PASSED OVER

Benjamin tried to hide his terror. But how could anyone be calm when the Angel of Death was scheduled to make an appearance? His older brother, Joshua, had started warning him about the terrifying visitor a week ago.

"The Angel of Death is coming," Joshua would whisper, every chance he got.

Benjamin would cover his ears and shout, "Stop saying that! It's not true!"

"Oh, yes, it is," Joshua would say. "I know these things."

What made it all the more terrifying is that he'd heard part of the very same story from his parents. They'd been talking about it for weeks. So he knew it wasn't just something Joshua made up to scare him.

"Moses wanted to take the Israelites out of Egypt and free them from slavery," his dad said, telling the tale to Benjamin like it was a bedtime story. "But Pharaoh, who ruled Egypt, wouldn't let them go."

And then came the scary part. God told Moses that all his people should mark the doors of their homes with lamb's blood. That way, when the Angel of Death came to take the firstborn sons of the Egyptians, he would know to pass over the houses of the Israelites. After the angel left, Moses led his people out of Egypt.

"And that's the story of Passover," his dad said. "It's a wonderful time of celebration, with a special meal."

Benjamin tried his best to find lamb's blood, so he could protect himself and his family from the Angel of Death. But he lived far from the nearest store. And lamb's blood turned out to be one of the few things you couldn't order online.

The day before Passover, Benjamin told his mom, "We need to mark the door."

"What for?" she asked.

"To save us from the Angel of Death," Benjamin said.

His mom laughed. But as Benjamin fought the urge to cry, her face got serious. "Oh, hon, don't worry. That happened long ago, and it only happened once, to punish Pharaoh. The Angel of Death isn't coming. There's nothing to be scared about."

Benjamin tried to find comfort in those words. But Joshua insisted he had special information. "Last time, the Angel of Death took the firstborn sons," he said. "Those were the oldest boys, like me. But I'm safe. This time, he's collecting the youngest sons."

"That's me!" Benjamin said.

"Yup. Too bad, little brother," Joshua said. "I'll miss you."

Far too soon, Passover came. Benjamin's family gathered with his aunts, uncles, and grandparents. Everyone seemed happy. The table was filled with delicious-looking food that sent wonderful aromas into the air, including beef brisket, potato kugel, and incredible macaroons and chocolate brownies his aunt had baked. But dessert was a long way off. First, they had to eat the traditional items. Benjamin barely managed to eat anything. His stomach was so jittery, he was afraid it would run away from the rest of his body.

Run away!

That's when Benjamin knew what he had to do. According to everything he'd heard, the Angel of Death didn't hide in dark alleys or leap down on people from trees. He visited the houses of his victims. That was definitely part of the story, whether it was told by his parents or his older brother. So Benjamin decided he'd leave his house before the Angel of

Death came. All he had to do was stay out-doors until sunrise, and he'd be safe for an-other year. Maybe, if he was lucky, his mom would have another child by then, and he'd no longer be the youngest.

As he stared down at a half-eaten slice of brisket on his plate, he wondered whether it was even safe to stay in the house until after dinner. Joshua hadn't told him exactly when the Angel of Death was coming. It could be at any moment. Benjamin looked at all the people around the table. Nobody was paying any attention to him.

He slipped out of his seat, grabbed his jacket from the hook in the hallway, and headed for the front door. Happily, the rain that had darkened the sky all afternoon had finally stopped, so Benjamin didn't have to worry about getting wet while he waited for morning.

"Bye, Benjamin," Joshua shouted before Benjamin could escape. "Can I have your brownie?"

"Where are you going?" his dad asked.

"Out," Benjamin said, reaching for the doorknob.

"Not by yourself, and not during dinner," his dad said. "Especially not during this dinner. Didn't you pay any attention to the stories I told you?"

"Yes!" Benjamin yelled.

"Calm down," his dad said, using words that never worked on anyone who wasn't already fairly calm.

"I have to get away!" Benjamin screamed.

"I told you no," his dad said. "Go to your room!"

"But . . ." Benjamin couldn't find the words he needed.

"Now!" his dad said.

Benjamin went up the stairs to his room and slammed the door. *I have to get out of here,* he thought. He looked out his window at the front lawn. He was too far above the ground to get down safely. But he knew if he climbed up to the roof, he could cross over to the rear side of the house, and then drop down to the roof of the back porch. From there, he'd have no trouble reaching the ground.

He slid open the window, stepped onto the ledge, grabbed the gutter, and pulled himself up to the roof. It was steeper than he'd expected, and slippery from the rain, but he bent over for balance and started to make his way up the treacherous slope. As he reached the top, he heard a sound behind him, like flapping wings. Startled, he looked over his shoulder.

That was a mistake. Thanks to the sudden movement, he slipped and fell. He made a grab for the peak of the roof, but he couldn't hold on.

"Help!" Benjamin yelled as he slid down the slick roof toward the edge. He sped closer and closer to the gutter. Halfway down, his slide turned into a tumble. He screamed again, but nobody was close enough to hear him.

At the end of his tumbling slide, Benjamin

slipped over the edge of the roof. He made a panicked grab for the gutter, and caught it with one hand. He jerked to a stop, dangling two stories above the ground, nowhere near a window.

I'm okay, he thought, amazed that he'd managed to save himself. He reached up and grabbed the gutter with his other hand. *I can get back up on the roof.*

As he gathered his strength to haul himself up, the gutter started to pull away from the house. Old steel spikes screamed as they tore free of the wooden eaves.

Benjamin looked down. The sight of the ground far below, and the concrete walkway right beneath him, caused his stomach to tie itself into a knot. He looked up as a dark shape blocked the moonlight. A man stood in front of him on the roof, dressed in a black robe.

The robe must have had slits, because Benjamin could see large wings jutting out the back.

"No!" Benjamin shouted when he realized he wasn't facing a man.

The angel bent over and grabbed Benjamin's wrist in a grip that felt like a swirl of fire and ice. Benjamin tried to look the angel in the face, but his eyes couldn't focus on it.

"Are you the Angel of Death?" he asked.

"There is obviously no need for him here," the angel said.

"What?" Benjamin didn't understand.

"You were doing a perfectly fine job of heading toward death, all by yourself. There was no need for any angelical assistance. You might have a hard head, but it's no match for a two-story plunge onto concrete."

"I wouldn't have fallen if you hadn't startled me," Benjamin said.

"Yes, you would have," the angel said.

"How do you know?"

"Trust me. I know these things," the angel said.

"So, who are you?" Benjamin asked.

"The Angel of Life," the angel said as he

hoisted Benjamin onto the roof. "Let's get you back to your room."

"But my brother said . . ."

"Your brother is a mean little *nudnik* who enjoys making people suffer," the Angel of Life said. "I think maybe I'll ask the Angel of Stomach Flu to visit him." He led Benjamin across the roof and lowered him safely to the bedroom window.

"Can he get there before dessert?" Benjamin asked. "Joshua always hogs all the brownies."

"I'll make sure he does," the Angel of Life said. "And as for you, go on back to dinner. Your father feels terrible that he yelled at you."

"Are you sure?" Benjamin asked. He realized his appetite had come back.

"Trust me," the Angel of Life said.

"You know these things," Benjamin said, echoing the angel's words from before.

"I do," the angel said. In the unfocused swirl of his face, a smile flickered. "He'll be happy to see you. This is not a day for sadness." And with that, the Angel of Life flew off, leaving Benjamin to enjoy the rest of the Seder dinner, a large helping of brownies, and the pleasant sight of watching Joshua leap from his seat and make a mad dash for the bathroom before he could even start to eat dessert.

FIGURED OUT

"Clear your desks, it's test time," Mr. Verber said.

Matt shoved his books inside his desk and closed the lid. It didn't go all the way down. He pushed harder. It resisted for a moment. Matt pushed even harder. He was rewarded with the sound of cracking plastic.

"You may use your calculators," Mr. Verber told the class. He walked over to the window and lowered it, shutting out the noise that drifted in from the construction site down the street.

"Oh no." Matt groaned as he realized the

most likely source of the sound of destruction that had shot from within his desk. He lifted the lid of his desk and pushed aside the piles of books and papers. Sure enough, there was a big crack on the front of his calculator, right between the number keys and the display.

"Matt, pay attention please."

Matt looked up. "Sorry," he said to his teacher. He put the calculator on his desk and took the test paper from Mr. Verber.

Work, he thought as he turned the calculator on. *Please work.*

The display came up. But instead of the usual line of zeros, it flashed a series of random numbers. Matt punched the 0 key. Nothing happened. He tried the plus key, the clear-entry key, and then the equal key. The calculator didn't respond.

"Oh boy." He sighed as he looked at the first question on the test.

Joseph has 37 marbles. He puts them on a scale and discovers they weigh 8½ ounces. How much does one marble weigh?

Matt shook his head. He knew he had to divide 8½ by 37 to get the answer. It would take him forever to do the test by hand. Around him, he could hear the click of fingers tapping calculator keys. Out of habit, he reached toward the keys on his own busted calculator. It was worth another try. His hand froze an inch above the keys. The display had stopped changing. It showed a number. The number 8.5 was there, just as if Matt had punched it in.

"Weird," he muttered, moving his hand toward the divide key. Before he could press it, the display blinked. Then the number changed to 37. Then it blinked again and became 0.229729729, and stayed that way.

Matt grabbed a pencil and started to check

the answer by hand. As he wrote each digit, first the 2, then another 2 and then a 9, his hand started to tremble. Finally, he dropped the pencil. For a moment, he just stared at the calculator. Then he looked at the next problem on the test.

A train leaves Boston traveling at 67 miles per hour. How far will it have traveled after 75 minutes?

That problem was a bit tougher. Matt wasn't sure whether he should start by figuring out the speed in miles per minute. He moved his hand over the calculator. The number 75 appeared. It blinked, as if he'd hit one of the function keys, then he saw the number 60. Another blink, and the display showed 1.25. Matt realized that 75 minutes divided by 60 showed how many hours the train had traveled. Sure—seventy-five minutes was one and a quarter hours. The display changed to

6⁊, then became 83.⁊5. Matt wrote down the answer and went to the next question.

He was the first one to turn in his test.

"Did you double-check your answers?" Mr. Verber asked when Matt walked up to the teacher's desk.

"I was very careful," Matt said. He hurried back to his seat as an idea flashed through his mind. He picked up the calculator and thought about calling his friend Travis. A surge of excitement rushed through Matt as he stared at the display. It showed Travis's phone number.

For a while, Matt just held the calculator. Another thought seized him. Getting the calculator to show Travis's phone number was no big deal. Matt already knew it. But what about another number? He thought about his favorite musician. The number changed. Matt couldn't believe his luck. He was holding the number for Johnny Backslash, lead guitarist for Toasted Brain Chili.

"I'll take that," Mr. Verber said.

"But—" Matt gasped as his teacher grabbed the calculator.

"The test is now over. Please pay attention to the lesson," Mr. Verber said. He dropped the calculator into his desk drawer.

Matt tried to pay attention, but his mind swelled with the thousands of ways he could use the calculator. At the end of class, he went up to his teacher and asked, "Could I have my calculator back, please?"

"Do you promise to pay more attention in the future?" Mr. Verber asked.

Matt nodded. His teacher handed him the calculator. It was all Matt could do to keep from snatching the treasure from the man's hand. As calmly as he could, he took the calculator and walked from the room.

How hot is it outside? he wondered as he walked.

The display changed to ٦3.

Matt stepped from the building into the mild air. It definitely felt like the low seventies.

That was close, he realized, thinking about how his teacher had taken away this marvelous device. Matt promised himself he would never risk losing the calculator again.

He gazed at the display, wondering what to ask it next. Before he had any thoughts, the number changed to Ǝⁿ0Ꮞ. Matt paused for a moment, and tried to figure out what it meant. Then he shrugged and said, "How much is Uncle Carl going to give me for my birthday?"

The display changed to 25. "Not bad," Matt said. Uncle Carl had given him twenty dollars last year, so this was an improvement.

The display changed back to Ǝⁿ0Ꮞ.

Matt didn't worry about that. As long as he got the answers he wanted, he really didn't care what other numbers appeared. He tested it again, wondering about how much Mr. Verber weighed and how many points the Lakers would score in their next game. He got an answer each time. And after each answer, the display returned to Ǝⁿ0Ꮞ.

Matt's mind swam with a thousand ways to use the calculator. Sports scores, stock market results, lottery drawings, there was no limit. Dreaming of ways he'd become rich and famous, Matt stared at the calculator as he walked. It showed ∃∩0Ч. Something looked very familiar about the numbers, but also very wrong.

"Hey kid," someone shouted at him.

Matt ignored the shouts. There was definitely something familiar about the numbers.

"Kid!"

"That's it," Matt said. He turned the calculator upside down. The display of ∃∩0Ч, seen this way, became letters instead of numbers. The message was hOLE.

"Hole?" Matt said.

His foot met air as he took his next step.

Matt dropped the calculator as he fell into a hole. It wasn't a deep drop, but it knocked the wind out of Matt. He didn't care about that. He cared about the smashed pieces of plastic he felt beneath his knee.

"Hey, kid? You okay?" a man wearing a hard hat asked as he peered into the hole.

Matt nodded.

"You should pay more attention to where you're walking," the man said. "You went right past the barriers and warning signs." He reached down and gave Matt a hand.

Matt looked back into the hole at the shattered pieces of his calculator.

The man followed his gaze. "Forget that junk," the man said. "Those things are nothing but trouble. A person should do his own thinking. Don't you think so?" The man grinned and waited for a reply.

"But . . ." Matt stood. He had no answer for that question. He had no answers at all.

EASTER BOOGEY

It's an easy job. Anyone could do it," the Master of Holidays said.

"Then why don't you do it, yourself?" the Boogey Man asked.

The Master of Holidays winced and rubbed his left knee. "I would, but I've got this bad knee. And I'm very busy."

"It's really not my sort of thing," the Boogey Man said. "I specialize in scaring kids and making sure they don't try to sneak out of the house at night."

"And you're great at that," the Master of Holidays said. "But we're in a real jam. Fluffy quit, yesterday. She just walked off, right before Easter."

"Why?" the Boogey Man asked.

The Master of Holidays shrugged. "She said she'd developed an allergy to eggs. Whatever the reason, she left me without an Easter Bunny for tomorrow. We need you. I asked the Master of Myths, Legends, and Monsters if she could spare you for an evening, and she agreed."

The Boogey Man sighed. It looked like he was stuck with the job. "What, exactly, do I have to do?"

"Hide eggs," the Master of Holidays said.

"That's all?"

"That's all," the Master of Holidays said. "It helps to be clever about it. The eggs need to be hard to find, but not too hard. We want the youngsters to have a great time."

"What's so great about eggs?' the Boogey Man asked.

"They have marvelous surprises inside them," the Master of Holidays said. "You never know what you'll find when you open one up. It could be a piece of candy, a small toy, or some coins. That's part of the fun. Children love surprises."

"Surprises . . ." the Boogey Man said as a lovely idea trickled into his crafty mind. "You're right. That could be fun."

"Great!" The Master of Holidays leaped to his feet and clapped his hands together in delight.

"Your knee seems much better," the Boogey Man said. "Maybe you should be hiding the eggs, after all."

The Master of Holidays dropped back into his chair. "Sometimes I get so excited, I don't notice the pain." He winced and rubbed his right knee. "I definitely need you to do this. Just make sure there are lots of surprises."

"I'm good at creating unexpected experiences and tampering with reality," the Boogey Man said. He didn't add that the biggest surprise of the next day would be for the Master of Holidays.

As night fell and the Boogey Man placed the first egg, he grinned his scary grin and said to himself, "He'll never ask me for another favor." He worked hard, and he worked fast, but even so, he barely managed to finish the job before the sun rose and eager children ran outside to greet the hidden treasures of Easter morning.

The Boogey Man hovered in the shadows at the far end of a dead-end street, and listened for his favorite sound. And soon enough, it came, as he knew it would. Screams started destroying the peaceful calm of neighborhoods everywhere very early on Easter morning as children discovered the colorful hidden eggs and broke them open in search of wonderful treats.

There were eggs filled with wasps.

Surprise!

Some had dozens of tiny spiders.

Happy Easter!

Others had one large tarantula that barely fit inside the shell and was so happy to be set free it crawled up its rescuer's shirt to give them a grateful hug.

Say hi to your new pet!

A few very special and rather large eggs had rats. But not just any kind of rat. These were zombie rats. The Boogey Man was quite proud of them, since they combined two fears into one wonderfully horrifying package.

Just for you!

The screaming baby bats were another clever and highly successful creation.

Keep on hunting!

By the end of the day, it was an Easter no child would ever forget. That evening, the Master of Holidays tracked down the Boogey Man in his cave, where he was sitting by a cold, dead fireplace, reading scary stories by Edgar Allan Poe.

"That was horrifying," the Master of Holidays said.

"Indeed." The Boogey Man grinned, again.

"You will never ever be asked to do that again," the Master of Holidays said.

"Just as I'd planned," the Boogey Man whispered in a voice too soft to be heard. But then his grin flipped to a frown that shifted to a pout as he remembered the wonderful shrieks of terror that had decorated the morning. He hadn't wanted to take the job. He'd done everything he could to make sure he would never be asked to fill in for the Easter Bunny again. But now that he knew how much fun it was to think up special treats to hide in eggs, he wanted to surprise children every Easter. And every other holiday. He pictured the wonderful horrors he could stuff inside a Thanksgiving turkey, and the dreadful presents he could sneak into houses for any gift-giving occasion. But now, he'd been told he'd never get to do any of that.

"Never ever?" he asked, just to be sure.

"Never ever at all, and absolutely not," the Master of Holidays said. "Oh, and one more thing . . ."

"What?" the Boogey Man asked.

"Now that I've had a good look at what sort of work you do, I've decided we need to eliminate your position," the Master of Holidays said. "Children are smart enough not to need fake scares to keep them from doing something silly."

The Boogey Man stared at him, unable to speak.

"You are outdated, obsolete, and no longer necessary," the Master of Holidays said. "I spoke with your boss, the Master of Myths, Legends, and Monsters, and she agreed. You are no longer allowed to hide in closets, lurk under beds, creep through attics, slither across rooftops, or in any other way disturb the nights or ruin the sleep of young children." With that, he left the cave.

The Boogey Man moped, sulked, whined,

moaned, and possibly shed a tear or two. But then his eyes fell on the object he'd been holding, and he realized there was still one way he could keep doing what he did best. Not only did he love scaring children, but he thought being safely scared was an important part of their lives. While he could no longer creep through the night, he knew there was more than one way to strike terror into young hearts.

He took a pen and a notebook—for he was truly a relic of the past—and started writing the opening line of the scariest story he could think of:

They teased Riley Shreager because he was an easy target. He was small, round, soft, and rather pale, with large, moist eyes that led to him being called owl face *or* bug boy *by the meaner kids in his class. Even the nicest students avoided him. None of the taunts seemed to bother him. Or if they did, he kept his feelings to himself.*

The Boogey Man was smiling again, now,

as the terrifying tale poured out of him. This was perfect. He could scare countless young readers without ever leaving the discomfort of his cold, damp cave. He'd always wanted to be a writer. And now, he had his chance . . .

THE INVENTION
OF MOTHERS

They teased Riley Shreager because he was an easy target. He was small, round, soft, and rather pale, with large, moist eyes that led to him being called *owl face* or *bug boy* by the meaner kids in his class. Even the nicest students avoided him. None of the taunts seemed to bother him. Or if they did, he kept his feelings to himself.

This lack of response only fueled the actions of the two worst bullies, Norbert Klezner and Andrea Vanderwitz. They mocked, taunted, and teased Riley anytime they could get away with it. All the teachers worked hard to prevent bullying, but every teacher has a dozen goals to accomplish throughout the day, or perhaps a thousand, while a bully usually has just one task in mind.

Things grew worse as Mother's Day approached. The students at Elmore Leonard Elementary School always put on a special play for their mothers, or other female guardians, the Friday before Mother's Day. (Fathers got a similar treatment right before the end of the school year.)

As everyone in the school who wasn't in the play filed into the auditorium, Norbert slipped behind Riley and whispered, "Where's your mother, you little worm?" He put his hand above his eyes like he was shielding them from the sun, and scanned the auditorium. "I don't see anyone ugly enough to be related to you."

Riley didn't respond.

"He's not a worm," Andrea said. "He's an owl. But not a wise one."

"Maybe his mother had to stay home with her eggs," Norbert said.

Riley's mouth twitched, like he was about to say something. But he remained silent, and managed to slip out of range of Norbert and Andrea when he took his seat. That was probably a good thing, since the play this year was about diversity and how there were all sorts of families, which would have given the bullies even more fuel for their taunts, because they didn't like anyone who wasn't exactly like themselves.

But just as Riley's luck would have it, they spotted him on Sunday morning, by the flower shop on Bachman Ave. Norbert and Andrea pretty much always hung out at the tiny corner market across the street from the shop because their parents pretty much always told them to stop horsing around and go play outside.

"Look who crawled out from under a log," Norbert said, pointing toward Riley, who was just entering the flower shop.

"Maybe he really has a mother," Andrea said.

Several minutes later, after a series of customers left the store holding bouquets of various sizes, Riley emerged clutching a single pink carnation as if it were a rare and delicate treasure.

"How pathetic," Norbert said. "One stupid little flower." He didn't add that he'd failed to get his own mother anything. Though it did occur to him that he had an easy shot at a carnation, if he wanted it. Not that he did.

Andrea, who had also been far from the best daughter, and ended up scrawling a Mother's Day card on a napkin with a crayon at the last minute, laughed. "What a loser."

"We have to see where he's going," Norbert said.

"For sure," Andrea said. "This should be interesting."

They waited until Riley was half a block away, and then followed him.

Riley, who seemed unaware he was being followed, walked past the last block of houses in town, turned off the main road, and headed down a narrow road with fields on one side and woods on the other.

"Maybe he lives in a tent," Norbert said.

"Or a tunnel," Andrea said.

It turned out she was right. Riley cut away from the road and headed into the woods, following a barely visible trail. About two hundred yards in, he knelt and lifted a flap that covered an entrance.

He went inside.

Norbert and Andrea exchanged glances. This was stranger than they'd expected, and a bit creepy. They both wanted to leave, but neither wanted to be the one who suggested they go back home. So they tiptoed to the edge of the hole, where a steep slope ran into the darkness beneath the ground, but they went no farther, at first.

Down below, they heard Riley say, "Happy

Mother's Day, Mom! I brought you a present."

Curiosity beat caution. Norbert and Andrea each took a single step forward.

That turned out to be one step too far. Slimy hands grabbed their ankles and yanked them into the tunnel. More hands grabbed them from all sides and carried them deeper under the ground. The darkness finally gave way to light when they entered a chamber where green, glowing moss coated the walls. Norbert and Andrea might have been happier if they hadn't seen what awaited them.

Creatures the height of toddlers surrounded them. They looked like eyeless worms with three pairs of arms and one set of legs. Past them, dominating half of the cavern, a bug that looked like Riley, if Riley had been inflated to twenty times his size and painted with buckets of slime, stared down with five pairs of insect eyes above a mouth filled with tiny black teeth.

Beneath this monster an egg the size of a beach ball emerged with the sound of a shoe being pulled free of mud. Workers carried the egg to a pile of other eggs. The eggs all pulsed, as if eager to hatch.

"See, I do have a mom," Riley said. "You were right, Norbert. She's sitting on eggs. And I have lots of brothers and sisters." Riley pointed to the creatures who were holding Norbert and Andrea. "They haven't gone into their cocoons yet. When they come out, they'll look like me."

Norbert and Andrea were now too terrified to think. The creatures dragged them toward Riley's mom, who opened her mouth, but not to speak.

"I love you, Mom," Riley said. He tossed the carnation aside. "I hope you like what I brought."

As the carnation hit the ground, Norbert

and Andrea realized that the flower wasn't the present. The flower was a trick to get them to follow Riley.

They were the present. And, ironically, that present had no future.

ABOUT THE AUTHOR

DAVID LUBAR credits his passion for short stories to his limited attention span and bad typing skills, though he has been known to sit still and peck at the keyboard long enough to write a novel or chapter book now and then, including *Hidden Talents* (an ALA Best Book for Young Adults) and *My Rotten Life*, which is currently under development for a cartoon series. He lives in Nazareth, Pennsylvania, with his amazing wife, and not too far from his amazing daughter. In his spare time, he takes naps on the couch.

ABOUT THE ILLUSTRATOR

BILL MAYER is absolutely amazing. Bill's crazy creatures, characters, and comic creations have been sought after for magazine covers, countless articles, and even stamps for the U.S. Postal Service. He has won almost every illustration award known to man and even some known to fish. Bill and his wife live in Decatur, Georgia. They have a son and three grandsons.